There's more to discover with Curious George!

Curious George DiSCOVERS the Senses

Adaptation by Adah Nuchi
Based on the TV series teleplay
written by John Loy

Houghton Mifflin Harcourt

Boston   New York

Photographs on cover and pp. 1, 3, 4, 8, 12 (top), 16 (bottom), 17, 18, 19 (kids), 20, 22, 24, 26, 30, 31 (left), 32 (left) courtesy of HMH/Carrie Garcia

Photographs on pp. 9, 11 courtesy of HMH/John Whittle

Photographs on pp. 16 (top), 19 (food), 31 (right) courtesy of HMH/Guy Jarvis

Photograph on p. 32 (right) © Park Street Photography/Houghton Mifflin Harcourt

All other photographs © Houghton Mifflin Harcourt

ISBN: 978-0-544-50026-6 paper over board

ISBN: 978-0-544-50023-5 paperback

Design by Susanna Vagt

www.hmhco.com

Printed in China

SCP 10 9 8 7 6 5 4 3 2 1

4500535517

Have you ever been curious about the five senses? You know—sight, sound, smell, taste, and touch? George is too! Come along as he discovers what they're all about!

In the country, things moved at a slower pace. Except for the man with the yellow . . . helmet! He was training for a triathlon race on Saturday. George was helping by keeping time.

Did you know . . .

a triathlon is a three-part race made up of swimming, cycling, and running? It takes a lot of time and energy to train for a triathalon. Which part of the race do you think would be the hardest? Which part would you be best at?

While the man was training, the roof of George's house was being repaired. When George and the man got home, the roof repairman told them, "The hole is bigger than we thought. A lot of water got in."

The hole was right above their bedrooms. Until it was fixed,
they had to move their beds downstairs into the living room.

George was excited to sleep in the living room.

It would be an adventure!

But George discovered that there are also problems with sleeping somewhere new. Especially after dark! In the dark, everything looked and sounded different. It made it hard for George to sleep.

Then something else made it hard for George to sleep—bats! George woke up to the sound of bats screeching in the dark.

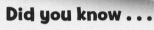

The bats woke the man up too. "They must have come in
through the hole in the roof," he said. The man tried to get the
bats out of the house, but he tripped over something in the dark.
"I wish I were a bat! Then I could get around in the dark too."
George was curious.

"Like us, bats can't see very well in the dark. They use their ears instead of eyes," the man explained. "Bats screech to find out where they are. Their voices bounce off of things so they know where things are even if they can't see. They use their sense of sound to hear where they're going."

Did you know . . .

the term for how bats find their way around in the dark is echolocation? Bats have the best hearing of all land mammals. They often have huge ears compared to the rest of their body. Bats make sounds and listen for the echoes when their sounds bounce back. Those echoes help them locate nearby objects and figure out how close they are. Another animal that uses echolocation is the dolphin.

Once the bats were out of the house, the man gave George a glass of milk to help him sleep. "You remember the five senses, George: sight, sound, taste, touch, and smell! We see with our eyes, hear with our ears, taste with our mouth, touch with our hands and skin, and smell with our nose."

"Do you think you can sleep now, George?" the man asked. George could. He went right back to sleep.

But the man didn't. The next day, he looked really tired during triathlon training. With the race only two days away, the man needed to get plenty of sleep to help keep his energy up.

Did you know . . .

your body needs sleep to help recharge from the day's activities? But sleep is also very important for your brain! Some scientists believe that your brain uses the time you're asleep to store information and solve problems. When you don't sleep enough, your brain doesn't work as well.

George hoped the man would sleep tonight. And he did.
But George was still wide awake! He needed another
glass of milk to help him fall asleep.

George didn't want to wake the man up by turning on the light, so he tried to find his way to the kitchen in the dark. But he kept bumping into things. Then George remembered what the man told him about bats. George thought he could use his voice and his sense of hearing to find his way in the dark too.

He tried screeching like a bat, but he couldn't hear his voice bounce off anything. He tried a little louder . . . and a little louder . . .

"What are you doing?" cried the man. All that screeching had woken him up.

Explore further:
Humans might not be able to hear as well as bats, but we can still use sound to figure out the distance and location of an object. Next time you're outside, close your eyes for a minute. What sounds do you hear? Can you tell where they're coming from? Can you tell if they are close to you or far away?

The next day, George felt awful. He'd kept the man up again. If only he had a way to quietly find his way to the kitchen in the dark. He couldn't see or hear his way. Then George got an idea while eating his breakfast—maybe he could taste his way to the kitchen!

George put some oatmeal on the floor. He could use it to make a trail.

"George!" The man cried out to stop him. Eating off the floor is never a good idea! If George couldn't use taste, sight, or sound, what senses were left?

Did you know . . .

that we often use many senses at one time? In fact, 80 percent of what we experience as taste is actually smell.

Oatmeal might not belong on the floor, but it does belong in a curious monkey's tummy. George took a deep breath in. It smelled good. If he left the oatmeal out, would he be able to smell his way to the kitchen? Just then, the man came over. "Want some honey with your oatmeal?" he asked George.

The honey was sticky, and that got George thinking. Maybe he could use touch!

George spread a honey path out along the floor. If George felt the honey with his feet, he'd know if he was going the right way. He was so excited about his path, he could hardly wait to try it out.

That night, when George couldn't sleep, he used the honey path to help find the kitchen. The honey was working. He was finding his way with touch!

But now the honey was stuck to George's feet. It was hard to find the path because it felt like the honey was everywhere.

"George? What are you doing?" the man asked.

Oops! George had woken his friend up again.

The next day, George decided to feel his way to the kitchen using something soft, not sticky. George looked in his toy box. Maybe he could use his stuffed animals! George's soft path had to work, because the man's race was tomorrow and he needed to get some sleep.

George's stuffed animals would tell him where the furniture was, but he needed more soft things to lead him to the kitchen. So, George rolled up some towels to make a path.

The man was so tired that he went to bed early. George didn't even have to wait until his bedtime to try his soft path out. Using his hands and feet, George worked his way to the kitchen. And he made it all the way without waking his friend up!

That night, George used his path many, many times. Since he was so excited about the man's race tomorrow, George was the one who couldn't sleep.

The next morning, George was there to cheer the man on as he swam . . . and rode . . . and ran his way to the finish line. But George missed the finish!

Because all that walking around at night made a monkey very sleepy.

Exploring the Senses:
SIGHT SOUND TASTE TOUCH SMELL

We use our five senses to understand our environment. Our senses work together to send information to our brain, and help us experience what's around us in lots of ways. We're always using at least one of our five senses!

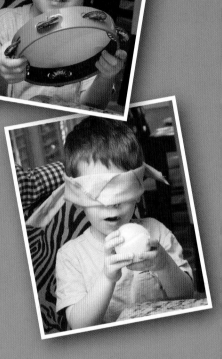

Test it out!

George had to rely on one of his other senses to help him find the kitchen because it was too dark to see. How good are your senses when you can't see?

You will need . . .

- a parent or friend
- several objects from your home
- a blindfold

What to do:

Ask your parent or friend to gather several objects around the house. (Don't look at them!) Cover your eyes with a blindfold. Using sound, touch, and smell, try to identify each item. Did you use different senses for each object? Which of your senses was most helpful in figuring out what each object was?

Extra challenge: You can make this experiment more challenging by gathering objects that are all about the same shape and size. Do you still use the same senses to figure out what everything is?

Taste Test!

It's no secret that holding your nose helps mask the taste of things. That's because 80 percent of what we experience as taste is actually coming from what we're smelling.

You will need . . .

- **several different flavored drinks, such as juices, water, and milk**
- **a cup for each drink**

What to do:

Fill each cup with a different flavored drink. Close your eyes and hold your nose. Ask a parent or friend to hand you the drinks one by one. Can you tell what's in the cup? Now keep your eyes closed and taste the drinks in the same order without holding your nose. Did you identify them correctly?

Figure it out

Our taste buds tell us if what we're eating is salty, sweet, bitter, sour, or savory.

Look at the foods pictured below. Can you figure out which taste category they belong in? If you're not sure, you might want to gather your supplies and start tasting!

SALTY

SWEET

BITTER

SOUR

SAVORY

Answer Key:
grapefruit = bitter, ice cream = sweet
pizza = savory, pickle = sour, popcorn = salty

Keep in Touch!

We experience our sense of touch over our whole body, but some areas have more touch receptors, or sensors, than others and therefore are more sensitive. Test out which areas are the most sensitive!

You will need:

- **two cotton swabs**
- **a friend**

What to do:

Have your friend close his or her eyes. Holding the cotton swabs close together, gently press them into the back of your friend's hand. Can your friend tell if you are pressing one or two cotton swabs? If your friend feels only one, try holding them a little farther apart. How far apart do the cotton swabs need to be before both are felt? Repeat this experiment on other parts of your body, such as the forehead, shoulder, back, upper arm, inner wrist, back of knee, fingertip, and foot. What areas are the most sensitive? Where is it easiest to feel two cotton swabs? Where do the cotton swabs need to be far apart to tell that there are two?

Words to Know

bitter: having a strong and often unpleasant flavor that is the opposite of sweet.

echo: a repetition of a sound that has bounced off a surface, such as a wall.

echolocation: a process for finding faraway or invisible objects by bouncing sound waves off objects so that they echo back to the sender, such as a bat's screech bouncing off its prey.

environment: the combination of land, weather, and living things that belong to a certain area.

nerve: a part of a system in your body (called the nervous system) that connects to other organs and sends messages to your brain so that you can move and feel.

nocturnal: being awake at night and asleep during the day; bats and raccoons are nocturnal.

predator: an animal that hunts other animals for food.

receptor: a nerve ending that senses changes in light, temperature, pressure, etc., and causes the body to react in a certain way.

saliva: the clear fluid in your mouth that helps you taste, chew, and swallow.

savory: a pleasant flavor that is most similar to salty, without being too salty or at all sweet.

screech: a high-pitched sound, like that made by a bat.

senses: sight, smell, taste, touch, and sound. These are the ways in which our body understands the world around us!

sensitive: being particularly aware of a sense, such as touch.

sensor: similar to a receptor; a part of your body that notices changes in heat, light, sound, motion, etc., and then sends the information to your brain.

taste bud: one of the receptors on your tongue that tells you how food is flavored.

tone: a sound of specific quality or pitch, such as high or low.

triathlon: a three-part race usually made up of running, swimming, and biking.